# Lil' Leo
## The Journey Begins

Written by
**Parnita Senjit**

I dedicate this book to all the adorable furry friends
around the world who bring joy into our lives.

Thanks to my husband Sandeep and my son Yash,
your encouragement and support has been priceless.

Thanks to Leo, he has been my primary source of inspiration,
we cannot imagine a single day without him.
**So, this is for you, Leo forever.**

Published in association with
Bear With Us Productions

**© 2021 Parnita Senjit**
**Lil' Leo The Journey Begins**
**www.parnitasenjit.com**

Cover design by Richie Evans
Design by Luisa Moschetti

**www.justbearwithus.com**

Illustrated by
**Novel Varius**

**Lil' Leo**
The Journey Begins

Written by
**Parnita Senjit**

It's another winter morning on the farm.

**I am excited!!**

"The Smiths are here!" the farmer's wife calls.
"They're here to take you home with them!
Do you remember them, Leo?"
**"I do, and there is Harry!"**

I wag my tail and hide behind my mom Lily.

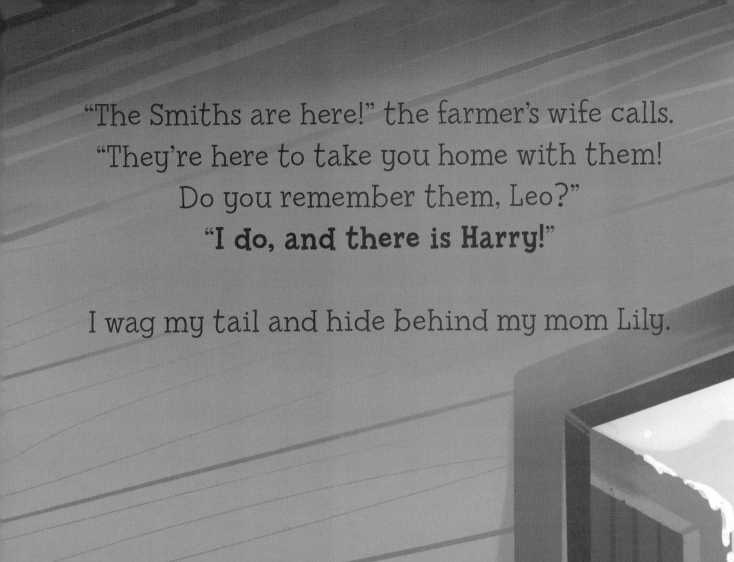

**"There you are, my little Leo!**
How have you been, I have been up all night
waiting to see you" says Harry.
I sit quietly feeling his warmth.

"It's time to say goodbye.
Take this blanket, it will remind Leo of his home,"
says Mom to Mrs Smith.

# "Where is everyone?" I ask.

"There is **Bella** near the
well with her bell,"
Mom tells me.

"And there is **Shep** by the moat, showing off his furry coat."

"Look at **Chicketty** with her chicks, all lined up clickity-click."

"There is **Casper**
near the plough,
taking a bow!"

"And there are **your
brothers and sisters**
near the shed, just
waiting for the
moment ahead!"

"And there's **Quicker**! Next to **Dad**.
Oh boy, he looks sad.

Don't worry, I will leave
today but I'll visit again another day!"

My new family take me to their car.

**My best friend Lucky is watching.**
I settle into a basket lined
with my blanket and wave goodbye.

"There's the scarf around my L'il Leo,"
Harry says.

I wonder what the scarf is all about.
Harry gave it to me at his last visit.
The car moves.

**"I won't leave you!"**
Lucky calls after us.

I feel the scarf on my neck.
Will I find out what it's for?

My tummy churns.

"Oh no! This is **not my farm, not my barn**!
The houses look big and the trees look
small! This is not my farm, not my barn!"

"Shh, it's okay, Leo, **I'm by your side**,"
Harry says.

**"We're here!"**
Mrs Smith says as we arrive at a bungalow.
**"Welcome to your new home!"**

The Smiths show me around the garden.
"It smells different, **not my farm, not my barn!**"

Harry takes me inside. I sniff the lounge.

I notice a strange decorated tree in the corner of the room. I am about to squat to pee when Mrs Smith picks me up. **"No, you don't pee inside!"**

**"**Going forward, let's get you to **nudge this bell** with your nose every time you have to go pee and I will take you outside,**"**

Mrs Smith explains, showing me a bell.
"Then we won't have any accidents inside."

**It's very different.**
Definitely **not my farm, not my barn.**

When evening comes,
there are loud bangs outside.

"It's okay, they are fireworks,
they won't harm you."
**Harry cuddles me.**

The beautiful twinkly lights of the tree in the corner catch my eyes. "That's our Christmas tree!" Harry says.

I bound over to it and sniff. I wag my tail and... **Oh no! I'm stuck.**

"Come here." Mrs Smith untangles me
from the lights and sits me on her lap.

"I know everything has changed and seems
very different, but you will soon feel
at home here, and we will look after you.
**How about I tell you a story?**"

There was a new boy at Harry's school.
His name was John. He was very nervous because
the school was so much bigger than he was used to.

"Boys and girls, who will be
John's buddy today?"
the teacher asked.

**Harry put his hand up quickly.**

Harry spent the week
helping John settle into school.

He showed him
around the
classrooms,

the playground
and the dining hall.

They spent a lot of time together, but
Harry noticed that John was always very quiet.

"What's wrong?" Harry asked.

**"I miss my friends and old school,"**
John explained.
"I don't like change."

**"I understand,"** Harry said.
"It's hard at first, but it will get better,
and you'll make lots of new friends."

When the boys walked home one evening
with John's mom, the sky grew darker
and the stars began to twinkle.

**"Wow! Look at those millions of stars!"**
John said.

Harry smiled and said:
"The stars make our night bright,
only then we know it is going to be alright."

"So, dear John, let's keep space for our old friends
and make room in our hearts for new ones!"

John's mom smiled
and thanked Harry for being so kind.

Over time, John was happier and made lots of friends. He loved his new school, but best of all he loved his new best friend - Harry. One day, John gave Harry a special present. **It was a black and white scarf!**

"This is for you Harry,
thank you for being there for me" says John

"Wow, thank you!" Harry said.
**"We will always be there for each other**
and have lots of fun!"

"Thank you! Thank you!"
I say to Mrs Smith as the story ends.
"I now know what my scarf stands for!
**It's a symbol of friendship and care"**

This was given to me when
Lucky and I became best friends!"

Now we all know what the scarf means
and why Harry gave it to me!"

**I relax, but I keep thinking about Lucky.**

Seeing me looking a bit lost, Harry runs into the room, saying, "Look here, Leo, look who is waiting to meet you!"

**"This is Bubba!"** Harry shows me a big old tortoise.

"Hello, Leo." Bubba smiles. "I've been looking forward to meeting you. You'll soon settle in, just like I did." Then the wise Bubba says: **"Let's embrace the change today so that we welcome yet another day."**

At bedtime I feel safe when Mrs Smith covers my pen with a blanket.

"It has started **feeling like my farm and somewhat like my barn.**

**But I do miss Lucky.**"

The next day is another fine morning.
"Come, let's play hide-and-seek, Leo!" Harry cries.
**I love hide-and-seek!** I used to play it
at the farm all the time.

"Come and find me!" Harry shouts.

## Sniff, Sniff.

"Are you under **the bed**,
eating your morning bread?"

"Are you behind **the door**, crouching on the floor?"

"Are you near **the curtain**, where I will find you for certain?"

"Or are you under **the table**, which reminds me of Casper's stable?"

Then the wise Bubba says:
"**Put your heart into what you've been searching for and you'll find more than you were expecting.**"

I sniff the air.
I follow the scent to my bed and...

"Wooaaaah, Lucky!"

My best friend Lucky is in my pen!

Now, it feels like my farm and
definitely like my barn.
My new home!

# Leo's Wisdom

Some of the sounds in your world are too loud and scary for me. In such situation, I may not know what to do, just like you.

💡 Tip: If a big noise or a bang scares me (like fire crackers), then cover my crate or take me by your side and we will listen to soothing music together. This will surely calm me down. I will feel more secure!

# Dog Alliance

Founder and Executive Director Debi Krakar
had a clear directive when establishing Austin Dog
Alliance in 2006. This Texas-based non profit
establishes dogs as an integral and integrated part of
communities by providing physical and mental health
benefits for children and adults.

Service dogs, therapy dogs, and the family pet all bring
tangible and positive changes to our lives ranging from
love and companionship to reduced heart disease, lower
blood pressure, and reduced stress & anxiety.

Therapy dogs like Leo use their social instincts and learned social skills to provide health, social-emotional, and cognitive benefits for individuals with specific challenges. As members of our Bow Wow Therapy Dog program, Leo and Parnita Senjit shared their positive attitudes and encouragement with children needing more confidence in reading. Leo's soft eyes and mere presence helps a child relax and be more receptive to learning.

This canine therapy team brought their warmth and smiles to senior citizens welcoming the companionship. Leo has been providing a calming influence for dementia patients. Although we label Leo as a "working dog," for him it is a natural extension of his personality and his innate connection with people.

**DOG ALLIANCE**

# Author

Parnita Senjit is a portrait artist, wellness coach and a motivational speaker. With deep interest in psychology through her university years, she is known to blend her experience & creativity in all aspects of her profession. In these challenging times, the introduction of a pet into the family has proved to be a comfort to many. At the same time, there has also been a tremendous increase in abandoned pets.

This backdrop provided the catalyst for the start of Parnita's literary journey. Basing her series of illustrated books on Leo, Parnita's stories are aimed at children and all those with a love or association with dogs.

Transforming her real-life certified therapy dog into a cartoon character that takes centre stage in her series of books, the author shares her learnings on how to understand, treat and get the most from your canine buddy.

Printed in Great Britain
by Amazon